For Taylor—M. B.

For grandmas Helen, Claudia, and Ruth—C. E.

Library of Congress Cataloging-in-Publication Data

Names: Barnett, Mac, author. | Ellis, Carson, 1975- illustrator.
Title: What is love? / by Mac Barnett ; illustrated by Carson Ellis.
Description: San Francisco : Chronicle Books, 2021. | Audience: Ages 3-5. |
    Summary: A boy sets out to find someone to answer a question that he
    asks his grandmother, and eventually his quest leads him back home.
Identifiers: LCCN 2021002780 | ISBN 9781452176406 (hardcover)
Subjects: LCSH: Love—Juvenile fiction. | Grandmothers—Juvenile fiction. |
    Picture books for children. | CYAC: Love—Fiction. |
    Grandmothers—Fiction. | LCGFT: Picture books.
Classification: LCC PZ7.B26615 Wh 2021 | DDC 813.6 [E]—dc23
LC record available at https://lccn.loc.gov/2021002780

Manufactured in China.

Design by Jennifer Tolo Pierce.
Typeset in Archer.
The illustrations in this book were rendered in gouache
on watercolor paper.

10 9 8 7 6 5 4 3 2 1

Chronicle books and gifts are available at special quantity
discounts to corporations, professional associations, literacy
programs, and other organizations. For details and discount
information, please contact our premiums department at
corporatesales@chroniclebooks.com or at 1-800-759-0190.

Chronicle Books LLC
680 Second Street
San Francisco, California 94107

Chronicle Books—we see things differently. Become part
of our community at www.chroniclekids.com.

WHAT IS LOVE?

by *Mac Barnett*

illustrated by Carson Ellis

chronicle books · san francisco

When I was a boy,
in the garden out front
of the house where we lived,
I asked my grandmother,

"What is love?"

My grandma was old.
I thought she would know.

She picked me up in her arms and said,
"I can't answer that."

"Who can?" I asked.

"If you go out into the world,
you might find an answer."

So I went.

I asked the fisherman,
"What is love?"

The fisherman smiled.

LOVE
IS A FISH.

"A fish?" I said.

"It glimmers and splashes,
just out of reach.
And the day that you catch it,
if you know what you're doing,
you give it a kiss

and throw it back in the sea."

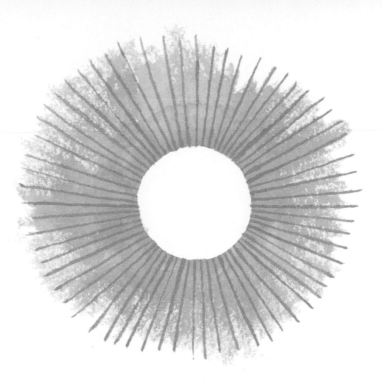

"But I don't like fish," I said.
"They're slimy and taste bad.
And they have creepy eyes."

The fisherman sighed.
"You do not understand."

I asked the actor,
"What is love?"

The actor smiled.

Love is

APPLAUSE.

"Applause?"

"It's the hoots of the crowd,
the sound of their hands.
You stand in the footlights
while they all scream your name.
Sometimes they throw flowers.
At that moment you know:
You exist. You are seen."

"But the crowd leaves," I said.
"They go home."

The actor sighed.
"You do not understand."

I asked the cat,
"What is love?"

The cat smiled.

Love is
the night.

"The night!" I said.
That sounded all right.

But before the cat could explain,
a dog chased it away.

"Wait!" I said. "Stop! What is love?"
The dog looked back and said,

I asked the carpenter,
"What is love?"

The carpenter smiled.

LOVE IS

"A house?"

"You hammer and saw,
and arrange all the planks.
It wobbles and creaks,
and you alter your plans.
But in the end, the thing stands.
And you live in it."

A HOUSE.

I said, "I'm not allowed to use hammers.
Once I busted my thumb."

"I don't mean a real hammer.
I'm not talking about thumbs."

"It got busted real bad."

The carpenter sighed.
"You do not understand."

The farmer told me love is a seed.

This soldier told me love is a blade.

That soldier told me love is a horse.

But the cart driver said, "No, it's a donkey."

A sports car, a donut, a lizard, a ring.
The first snow of winter, a maple in summer.
A grizzly bear, this pebble right here—
these are all things people told me love is.

I asked the poet,
"What is love?"

The poet smiled.

"Sit down and I'll tell you," he said.
"A list so long it goes on for pages."

I didn't have time to listen to that!

"Wait!" said the poet.
"I have not answered your question!"

"You sure haven't!" I said.

The poet shouted at me,
"You do not understand!"

And so one day I returned
to the house where we lived.

The lights were all on.
I smelled dinner cooking.
My dog barked gladly at me
from a window upstairs.

I took off my shoes
and I stood in the garden.
I curled my toes,
so they dug into the dirt.

I sighed.

I didn't hear my grandmother
come up behind me.

"Finally," she said.
"You have come back."

She was older.
I was taller.

She asked me,
"Did you answer your question?"

I picked her up in my arms.
I smiled.

I said,

Yes.